12/04

DISCARD

Star SCENE

Miley Mania!

Behind the scenes with Miley Cyrus

By Jackie Robb

New York   Toronto   London   Auckland   Sydney
Mexico City   New Delhi   Hong Kong   Buenos Aires

Front Cover: Sara De Boer/Retna Ltd.
Back Cover: Frank Gunn/The Canadian Press/AP Photo.

Page 1: George Taylor/Everett Collection. Page 3: Joel Warren/©Disney Channel/courtesy Everett Collection. Page 4: Jon Kopaloff/FilmMagic/Getty Images. Page 5: Michael Germana/Everett Collection. Page 6: (Top) Kathy Hutchins/Hutchins Photo/Newscom; (middle) Jon Kopaloff/FilmMagic/Getty Images; (bottom) Alex Blasquez/Retna. Page 7: (Top) Paul Smith/Featureflash/Retna; (bottom) Sara De Boer/Retna. Page 8: Sara De Boer/Retna. Page 9: Chris Polk/FilmMagic/Getty Images. Page 10: Michael Germana/Everett Collection. Page 11: (Top) Harper Smith/Retna; (bottom) Dee Cercone/Everett Collection. Page 12: © Frazer Harrison/AMA/Getty Images. Page 13: © Adam Nemser/PHOTOlink/Newscom. Page 14: Kristin Callahan/Everett Collection. Page 15: © Arnaldo Magnani/Getty Images 16: Rena Durham/Retna. Page 17: (Top) © Sara De Boer/Retna; (bottom) Scott Weiner/Retna. Page 18: Michael Germana/Everett Collection. Page 19: Karl Larsen/FilmMagic/Getty Images. Page 20: Michael Germana/Everett Collection. Page 21: Jon Kopaloff/FilmMagic/Getty Images. Page 22: Michael Tran/FilmMagic/Getty Images. Page 23: Michael Germana/Everett Collection. Page 24: Rena Durham/Retna. Page 25: Adriana M. Barraza/WENN/Newscom. Page 26: Sara De Boer/Retna. Page 27: Michael Germana/Everett Collection. Page 28: Russ Elliot/AdMedia/Newscom. Page 30: ZUMA Press/Newscom. Page 31: Sara De Boer/Retna. Page 32: Alex Blasquez/Retna. Page 33: Camilla Zenz/ZUMA Press/Newscom. Page 34: Rena Durham/Retna. Page 35: Byron Purvis/AdMedia/Sipa Press/Newscom. Page 36: © Harper Smith/Retna Ltd. Page 38: Dee Cercone/Everett Collection. Page 39: Kathy Hutchins/Hutchins Photo/Newscom. Page 40: Sara De Boer/Retna. Page 41: Aaron D. Settipane/WENN/Newscom. Page 42: Rena Durham/Retna. Page 43: Andreas Branch/PatrickMcMullan.com/Sipa Press/Newscom. Page 44: © Russ Elliot/AdMedia/Newscom. Page 46: Scott Weiner/Retna. Page 48: Dee Cercone/Everett Collection.

ISBN-10: 0-545-08565-9
ISBN-13: 978-0-545-08565-6

Published by Scholastic Inc.
SCHOLASTIC and associated logos are trademarks and/or registered trademarks of Scholastic Inc.

12 11 10 9 8 7 6 5   8 9 10 11 12/0

Cover Designed by Angela Jun
Interior Designed by Jenn Martino
Printed in the U.S.A.
First printing, May 2008

Introduction

When *Hannah Montana* first appeared on the Disney Channel in the spring of 2006, no one was prepared for the wave of *Montana*-mania that would soon be sweeping the country. The Disney Channel had already produced some smash shows, such as *The Suite Life of Zack and Cody*, *That's So Raven*, and of course, *High School Musical*. But there was something truly special about *Hannah* and its star, the bubbly Miley Cyrus, something that captured the imagination of fans across the USA.

Miley is no stranger to superstardom. Her dad, Billy Ray Cyrus (who just happens to play her TV dad, Robbie) had experienced it firsthand when he was a country singer in the 1990s. His country dance hit, "Achy Breaky Heart," had the whole country line dancing and singing along, and his pinup handsome face brought legions of fans to country music. Although Miley was just a baby when her dad was experiencing the height of his fame, she certainly had heard stories of her dad's awesome success.

But there was no way Miley ever could have imagined that she herself would become a household name and face, appearing on TV, singing on the radio, charting a No. 1 album of hits, and popping up on everything from T-shirts to lunch boxes.

Luckily, she's able to share her fame with her friends and family. She and her family are super-close, and her dad is always at her side — she loves having him as her costar and

appreciates all his help and guidance. She's also close to her mom, Tish, who always told Miley she could be anything she wanted to be. Miley spends lots of time with her TV (and real-life) best friend Emily Osment, and her costars Mitchel Musso and Jason Earles. Miley shared crushes with her TV alterego Hannah when Cody Linley and Jesse McCartney appeared on the show, and she

even briefly dated Nick Jonas, who, along with his brother Kevin and Joe, guest starred on a *Hannah* episode. Miley definitely believes in getting by with a little help from her friends!

So read on and catch all the facts about Miley, Hannah, and her friends. It won't be long before you're an absolute Miley know-it-all.

Miley Mania!

If you're Miley's #1 fan, you'll want to check out these amazing facts!

Head-To-Toe Fax

Full Name:	Destiny Hope Cyrus
Nickname:	"Smiley." She received her nickname from her dad, Billy Ray, who was amazed by his daughter's constant smile
Birthday:	November 23, 1992
Birthplace:	Franklin, Tennessee — just outside of Nashville
Family:	Her parents are Billy Ray and Leticia "Tish" Finley Cyrus. She has two older half-brothers, Christopher Cody and Trace, and an older half-sister, Brandi. Her younger siblings are brother Braison Chance and sister Noah Lindsey
Pets:	Dogs Loco and Tag, who live in Los Angeles. In Tennessee, Miley has horses, which live at her grandmother's house
Eyes:	Green-blue
Height:	5' 4"
Righty or Lefty:	Miley is right-handed

Miley's Fabulous Faves

Colors:	Pink and lime-green
Book:	*Don't Die, My Love* by Lurlene McDaniel
Singers:	Hilary Duff, Kelly Clarkson, and dad, Billy Ray
Food:	Ramen noodles, gummi bears, and anything Chinese
TV Shows:	*The Hills* and *Laguna Beach* — Miley loves reality TV!
Actors:	Sandra Bullock and Orlando Bloom
Drink:	Snapple and caramel frappuccinos
Gum:	Orbit
Season:	Summer
School Subject:	Math
Hobby:	Shopping — she loves Hollister and Nordstrom
Greatest Fear:	Flying. "It makes me nervous. It feels weird to know that you're in the air."

DID YOU KNOW . . . ?

Miley shares a birthday with *High School Musical's* Lucas Grabeel.

The Word on Her Costars

ON EMILY OSMENT:

Miley told *Bop!* magazine: "She's become one of my best friends, and we're rarely ever apart. When you're with someone all the time, it's more than being a friend; it's like you're sisters, and we're sisters now. There's nothing we can't say to each other, and I don't think I've ever really had a friend like that."

ON MITCHEL MUSSO:

Miley told *J-14* magazine: "Mitchel is one of the funniest guys I know, but I've also come to trust him very much. He's like a combination of best friend and brother. I've always had a lot of guy friends, and I like to get a guy's point of view on things, so I'm not afraid to ask him, 'Hey, do you like this outfit? Do you like my hair this way?'"

ON JASON EARLES:

Miley told *J-14* magazine: "On the show, he really seems crazy funny, but in real life he's one of the most serious people I've ever met. He's definitely more mature than his character lets on. He's another person who I trust. When you ask him a question, you know you're going to get a very thoughtful answer."

Miley knows that she is one very lucky girl — not only does she star in her own TV show, but her costars are some of her best friends. Here are some of the things she had to say about the actors who share the *Hannah* stage with her.

ON BILLY RAY:

Miley told *USA Today*: "What can I say? Working with my dad is a dream for me. I respect his talent and his creativity, so if he was just another actor, I would admire him. But he's also my dad, and I love him so much. He's a wonderful father, and I just can't believe I get to take this journey with him every day. The only negative is, when we're driving to work, my dad just talks and talks about the most random things, and he plays the most random music."

DID YOU KNOW . . . ?

One of Miley's best friends is Ashley Tisdale, from *High School Musical* and *The Suite Life of Zack and Cody*. "When we met, it was like, giggling from the get-go. It's like she adopted me as a little sister or something, and we're really attached at the hip. Of course, I get the benefit of that, 'cause I get all her hand-me-downs — she's got great clothes, and I get them 'cause I'm the little sister. And sometimes I even spend the night at her house, which I love because she has the greatest room in the world — it's like a seven-year-old's, with dolls and stuff. We do so much together — she's the best!"

EXPERT SHOPPER

Miley loves to shop; she's just wild about cool clothes, and she goes bonkers over shoes. Although she'll shop anywhere, she does have a secret shopping destination: Target. Miley revealed to *Bop!* magazine, "I love shopping at Target. The way clothing trends are, something comes out and it's really cool and you have to have it. And then a few months later you never want to look at it again. At Target, things aren't as expensive, so it isn't such a big deal if you wear it once, then never wear it again. You don't want to do that with more expensive clothes — at least I don't. I feel horrible when I buy something expensive, and then I have to tell my mom, 'Oh, I don't want to wear that anymore — it's old!'"

DID YOU KNOW . . . ?

Miley always wears a leather bracelet, given to her by her mom. She says it's her good luck charm, and she's rarely without it — if it's not on her wrist, it's somewhere in her pocket or purse.

FASHION PLATE?

Like Hilary Duff, her idol and role model, Miley may one day become a fashion designer with her own line of clothing. "We're discussing that right now!" she enthused to the audience at a *New York Times* interview session. "We want to put out all the Hannah clothing, all the fun stuff she wears. So many fans have asked, 'Where can we get Hannah's clothes?' and I think it would be totally cool if 'Hannah' herself designed them!"

DID YOU KNOW . . . ?

Miley has been quoted as saying, "Pink is not just a color, it's an attitude."

Miley Makes Her Entrance

On November 23, 1992, Destiny Hope Cyrus arrived to the delight of her parents, Tish and Billy Ray Cyrus. From the moment she was born, the tiny baby seemed to have a never-ending smile on her face. Although her parents named her Destiny Hope, believing she would one day accomplish wonderful things, they nicknamed her "Smiley," in honor of that constant grin. Eventually, the family took to calling her Miley, a shortened version of "Smiley."

Miley entered a family that was big, boisterous, and loving. There were three older half-siblings, Christopher Cody, Trace, and Brandi. And later on, two younger siblings would join the family, Braison Chance and Noah Lindsey. Billy Ray's parents, Ann and Ron, were doting grandparents, and Tish's mom, Loretta Finley, was an equally loving grandma.

Billy Ray was already a singing sensation in the country music world when Miley was born, and Miley quickly showed signs that she would also be attracted to music. During a Disney Channel press conference, the Cyruses described Miley's singing "debut." "When I was two, my dad brought me on stage and I sang 'Hound Dog' and other silly songs with him," she says. "It was just for fun, and my dad was really proud of me." Her dad remembers it differently. "She was supposed to be on the side of the stage," he laughs. "She would always escape from whomever was watching her, and if I was on stage singing, she would break free from her nanny or her mom, run on stage, and grab the nearest microphone. There was no way she wasn't meant for this business."

Miley attended Heritage Middle School in Franklin, and made many friends there, including her lifelong best friend, Lesley Patterson, who also remembers that Miley was always singing. Miley also tried out for the cheerleading squad at her middle school and made it. "I loved cheerleading, and it was an important part of my life," she says. So important, in fact, that she became a part of the Premier Tennessee All-Stars, a competitive cheerleading team. "It was hard work, let me tell ya!" she laughs. "I loved it, because it was just another way of expressing myself through performance. I loved winning trophies and being a part of the team — there were some great girls on the team, and we were really close, because we worked together so often."

When Miley was nine, she and her family traveled to Toronto to visit her dad at work — he was appearing on the show *Doc*, which was being filmed there. She was impressed by the way the actors all worked together, the way they laughed and talked during their breaks, and the way they supported each other. She never forgot her experience on the set and imagined that one day she would have the chance to work with such great people.

Even though Billy Ray had at first discouraged his daughter, he began to recognize how determined his little girl was. He also knew she was talented. And he could see that, as she got older, her dream of becoming a performer was growing. She had the passion.

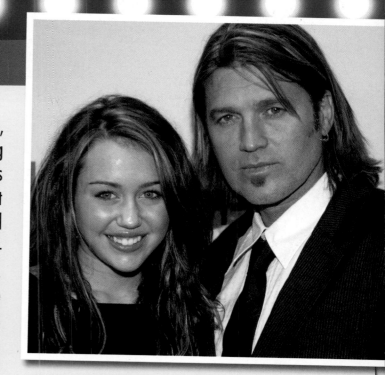

Miley began to study acting, and she got an acting coach to help her. She also continued singing, which she also loved, and practicing the guitar. She'd been playing since she was young, ever since her dad gave her a pink Daisy Rock guitar as a present. She started to practice on the instrument, happy to have received such a wonderful gift, and she soon became an excellent guitarist.

Miley's first role was a recurring one on the show *Doc*, with her dad. Then she began auditioning for other parts, and won the role of Young Ruthie in the movie *Big Fish*, directed by Tim Burton. But while she constantly went out on auditions, very often the answer she heard most was, "No." At the Disney Channel press conference, her dad reminisced about those hard days. "I saw that child go on so many auditions and get turned away. She just kept on keeping on and never gave up hope."

Even the role of Hannah Montana — a role that seems to be obviously meant for Miley — was not an easy one to get. Over 1,000 girls — some with acting experience, many with none — auditioned for the part, and Miley didn't get any special treatment just because she was Billy Ray Cyrus's daughter. Singers like JoJo and *American Juniors* finalist Jordan McCoy auditioned — JoJo got the role and rejected it — and actress Alyson Stoner was also a contender. Miley auditioned not only for Hannah, but for the role of Lily, Hannah's best friend. "I did not get the role right away — in fact, it was the total opposite of 'right away,'" Miley told reporters at the Disney Channel press conference. "I had to keep going back, over and over again. I kept thinking I had it, then I kept thinking I didn't. It was the hardest time for me — I wanted to stay positive, but sometimes I thought, 'I might as well give up!' But I kept going on, because I knew in my heart I was Hannah."

Eventually, Disney Entertainment President Gary Marsh came to realize that, too — especially after Miley offered to fly herself back out to Los Angeles to audition for the role one last time and to pay for her own plane ticket. He described his reaction to Miley at the Disney Channel press conference. "No one ever made that offer before," he joked. "We knew we couldn't go forward until we found someone who could carry the show, and honestly, we hadn't found that person yet. The last time I looked at Miley, I saw that she had something special. She's very natural, and she has wonderful comic timing. She had the qualities necessary to make her believable in this role, the ability to straddle the music world and the real-life world. And of course that voice — she has the most beautiful singing voice, perfect, just what we needed."

When Miley heard the news, she just about exploded with happiness. And she was even happier when she learned that her dad, Billy Ray, would be her co-star, something she truly hadn't expected. "I used to go to work with him, and now he goes to work with me!" she laughs. "I think we're both very thankful to be doing this together, and it's amazing to be a part of this."

FUN FACT ABOUT FRANKLIN, TENNESSEE!
For a small town, Franklin has produced a lot of famous folk. Singers Carrie Underwood, Jordan Pruitt, and Vince Gill hail from this southern spot, and actress Ashley Judd was also born in Franklin. As for the state of Tennessee, it's given birth to stars like Justin Timberlake, Reese Witherspoon, and, of course, Dolly Parton, whose theme park Dollywood is set in the Smoky Mountains.

The Hannah Montana Phenomenon

Hannah Montana is the story of a young girl who lives a normal, everyday kind of life with her family and friends, but has a very special secret — she's a rock star!

But that simple description doesn't tell the whole story. Hannah Montana has become one of the most popular shows on the Disney Channel. Fans across the country have fallen in love with the Stewart family and with Miley/Hannah, who belts out rock songs at night and works to get good grades during the day. The show's executive producer, Steve Peterman, believes he knows the secret to Hannah's success, and explained it saying, "I think everybody, at one time or another, has wanted to be a rock star. . . . But with Miley, you also have a girl who knows that being a celebrity is great, but that being with your family and friends is actually the more important thing in life. Miley knows how important it is to be with the people who really care about you."

Everyone involved with *Hannah Montana* agrees that another part of the show's amazing success lies within Miley Cyrus, the young talent that Disney almost didn't hire. "It was true that at first we didn't know if she could do it, hold the whole show together," says Peterman. "We thought, 'This is an enormous weight to put on someone's shoulders. Could she do it?' She was so young and about six inches shorter than she is now, and she looked like this little, tiny girl, and we wondered, 'Could she do it?' Then she opened her mouth and sang, and all the doubts began to disappear. You know, we didn't even know she was the daughter of Billy Ray Cyrus — no one made that connection — but of course once you hear her sing you know. It's in the genes."

Fans soon found they had a friend in Miley and Hannah, and they began tuning in each night to see what kinds of adventures their heroine would get into. On blogs and web pages across cyberspace, fans began to talk about their devotion to Miley. "She's like the best friend you want to have," wrote one fan. And that seems to be the main attraction Miley has for her fans — they see her as a best friend. "There's no one on TV right now who is like this girl," Peterman says of Miley. "She's able to make a connection with the audience, and they feel close to her."

Fans also loved Miley's relationship with her dad and brother. One blogger wrote, "What a great dad! I think he's got to be the best dad in TV. He's kind and considerate, and supports Miley and Jackson, but he's also a real guiding hand for them." Miley, who was thrilled to learn her dad would be her co-star, tells a secret about that family dynamic. "I get to get away with a lot of crazy stuff on the show, stuff I would never be able to get away with in real life. I got to pour Chinese food all over him. Once he got a load of cake in his face and I laughed like crazy. I sometimes tell him, 'Dad, you know I talk to the writers, and I make sure you get hit with something in every show.' That's a joke of course, but actually — I think he does get hit with something almost every week."

In addition to Miley and her dad, the show also has a collection of wonderful supporting actors who make it a fun and silly place to be. Actor Mitchel Musso was one of the first actors to be hired; he won the producers over with his winning sense humor. Emily Osment was brought on to play Lily, Miley's best friend, and she played the role so convincingly that she and Miley became BFFs in real life.

The last role to be cast was Jackson, Miley's goofy older brother. "At first, we thought Jackson was going to be the brother who had a problem with having a star for a sister," says Peterman. "At first, we had him using a ventriloquist's dummy, and we thought he would use the dummy to say the angry, kind of mean or jealous things he wouldn't be able to say to his sister's face. Jason Earles was hysterical — he was the only actor to make that dummy funny. But then we realized he was so funny he didn't need the dummy. So we got rid of the dummy and kept Jason."

And everyone on the show admits that Hannah's awesome music helps drive the series. The *Hannah Montana* soundtrack shot to number one on the music charts, and fans absolutely love the music she makes. "There's a wonderful energy to Hannah and her music," says Peterman. "It adds something to the show and makes it different. But then, the music is so good, I think Miley/Hannah would be just as popular if she only recorded music. It's great stuff."

What You Must Know About Mitchel

If you're craving the 411 on the actor who plays Oliver, you've come to the right spot.

Head-To-Toe Fax

Full Name:	Mitchel Tate Musso
Birthday:	July 9, 1991
Birthplace:	Garland, Texas
Family:	His parents are Samuel and Katherine, and he has two brothers, Marc and Mason. Little brother Marc was the first Musso to get into show business — he was modeling and doing commercials when Mitchel decided he wanted to give it a try as well
Pets:	A yellow labrador retriever called Stitch

Mitchel's Fabulous Faves

Color:	Blue
Actors:	Keanu Reeves and Jessica Alba
Sports:	Basketball, skateboarding, and snowboarding
Music:	Hip-hop and rock
Movie:	*Lord of the Rings*
Food:	Sushi
Candy:	Twix Bars and Skittles
TV Show:	*American Idol*

When Miley Stewart needs help and support, she knows she can always turn to Oliver Oken, one of her two best friends. In real life, Mitchel Musso, the actor who plays Oliver, and Miley have become great friends. "For some reason, before the show started, I always had more guy friends than girlfriends," Miley admitted to *Tiger Beat* magazine. "I always had a pretty easy time making friends with guys. With Mitchel, I found a friend who definitely knows how important it is to be honest and straightforward. You know where you stand with Mitchel. And he's great at giving me advice, you know, the kinds of advice you need when you're a girl and you're meeting guys you like? Mitchel is a great sounding board. I'm afraid he's had to listen to a lot of my chatter about guys, and he always gives me the best advice in the world."

Mitchel began his acting career in 2002 when he appeared in TV movies called *The Keyman* and *Am I Cursed?* But he'd been bitten by the acting bug at a much younger age. "I was about nine when I first started thinking about it," he told *J-14* magazine. "If you can believe it, it was my younger brother Marc who convinced me to try it. He was doing a lot of modeling and appearing on commercials, and when he appeared on his first TV commercial and I saw it, I thought, 'Whoa, is that the coolest thing ever? That's my brother on TV!'"

Once Mitchel began to audition for roles himself, he found quick success, appearing in lots of TV roles in shows like *Walker, Texas Ranger* and other TV movies. He also nabbed a role in the feature film *Secondhand Lions*, and provided the voice of DJ in the 2006 hit movie, *Monster House*. "That was a lot of fun, and something that was an amazing experience," he says. "It was quite exciting, being in a movie that was so successful. It was crazy. My little brother is always after me to do the voice, but then when I do it too often, he tells me to stop it."

Although he admits it isn't as easy for many young actors just starting out, he found his early acting career moved very smoothly. "I was ten or eleven when I went out on my first audition," he says. "I got the first thing I auditioned for. I didn't really think about being rejected, but now it hits me, how crazy everything works. But when I started, I wasn't thinking about getting rejected — it was just my life, and I just went about doing it."

There was no doubt that Mitchel was the man to play Oliver — he auditioned for the role, and became one of the first actors hired for the show. "Oliver is kind of goofy — he calls himself 'Smokin' Oken' and things like that," Michael said to *J-14* magazine. "He is best friends with Lily and Miley, and he's really all about girls and his style. Lily and Miley are always helping him, setting him up with girls and trying to help him find his 'Miss Right.' I definitely like him — although I think he's a little sillier than I am. But I have to admit, he has some pretty slick moves when it comes to the girls. I think I may be learning from the best when it comes to meeting girls!"

As soon as he met Miley and Emily Osment, he knew he'd found a home away from home on the set of *Hannah Montana.* "They are my greatest friends, and we laugh all the time," he says happily. "Miley is really jumpy and perky, and loving and nice to everyone. Emily is the sweetest girl, and I can talk to her about anything. We have the greatest cast and crew, truly I could not wish for anything better. When you walk in, you immediately get the vibe that this is your second home."

And thanks to his success on *Hannah,* Mitchel has also nabbed another Disney show role — he and Ashley Tisdale of *High School Musical* will be voicing characters in the new Disney animated show, *Phineas & Ferb.* "We go in every other Tuesday, and we record two episodes when we go in," Mitchel explains. "I play a regular on the show named Jeremy, and Ashley plays a main character, the sister of Phineas and Ferb. It's a lot of fun because Ashley and I know each other and we have fun together. It only takes a couple of hours, and it's an awesome project, so I'm glad I have the chance to do something like this. Maybe I'll become a major 'voice' in animated films — I would love that."

In addition, Mitchel is filming a new pilot for Disney called *Mascot Prep,* a show where he would be the star. Mitchel says, "It's a cool story — that's all I'm going to say right now because I don't want to bring bad luck. But there are some great people in it, and I think it could be really funny. We shot the pilot and we're adding a couple of new things, so I'm looking forward to people seeing it and hearing what they think."

While Mitchel knows that he wants acting to be his career, he also intends to go to college soon, and he looks forward to that part of his life as well. "I definitely want to go to college, and I already have the college money put aside," he says. "I want to take a lot of business courses concerning money. I definitely want to make sure I know how to handle money. A lot of actors make the mistake of thinking they'll always have a ton of money, but I know how important it is to handle money properly, and I want to learn how."

Pretty serious stuff from goofy Oliver! "Don't let him fool you," Mitchel joked to *J-14* magazine. "I think he's pretty serious about certain things, too. It's just that for right now, he's all about having fun and meeting girls — which honestly is what I'm about right now too!"

DID YOU KNOW . . . ?

Mitchel and his two brothers all have the initials MTM.

All About Emily

She's Miley's BFF —
could she be yours, too?

5' 4" 5' 4"

Head-To-Toe Fax

Full Name: Emily Jordan Osment
Birthday: March 10, 1992
Birth Place: Los Angeles, California
Family: Parents are Eugene and
                Theresa; her older
                brother is Haley Joel,
                whose performance
                in the creepy film
                The Sixth Sense won him an Oscar nomination
Height: 5' 2½"
Eyes: Blue
Pets: Golden retrievers named Tor and Nado, and various turtles,
                fish, and lizards
FYI: Emily is scared of heights

Emily's Fabulous Faves

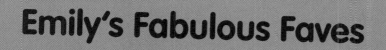

Color:	Blue
Hobby:	Knitting — she taught Miley and now they both love it — and cooking
School Subjects:	English and literature
Actors:	Tom Hanks, Jake Gyllenhaal, and Audrey Hepburn
Food:	Bell peppers and anything Italian, especially ravioli
Dessert:	Cheesecake
Sports:	Soccer — she's played since she was six years old — and swimming

If you have older brothers and sisters, you know it isn't unusual to look up to them, to ask them for their advice, and to view them as role models for your future. That's exactly what happened in the Osment household when little Emily Osment realized that her big brother Haley Joel was a big star in the movie world. He'd received an Oscar nomination for his role as the sad, lonely boy who "sees dead people" in the huge film hit *The Sixth Sense*, and he had been appearing in movies for most of his young life. "In a way, I think I was always trying to be just like him," she told *J-14* magazine. "When we were little, people always used to ask us, 'Who's who?' because we looked so much alike and we still do. I think in my heart I was always trying to do what he was doing and to be just like him, because I always admired him so much."

When Emily was six, she began to pursue her dream with all the determination of a pro. In 1998, she won the role of Miranda in the movie *The Secret Life of Girls*, and that same year she appeared in the TV movie *Sarah, Plain and Tall: Winter's End*. Four years later, in 2002, Emily was back, voicing an animated character in *Edward Fudwuper Fibbed Big*, and making a huge splash as Gerti Giggles in *Spy Kids 2: Island of Lost Dreams* (a role she reprised in 2003 in *Spy Kids 3-D: Game Over*). Emily was thrilled to be a part of the *Spy Kids* films, and she told *USA Today* about some of the crazy stunts she was involved in during the filming. "At one point I was hanging off a cliff. There were sharp rocks and I was in a harness. I've rock climbed before and I'd been in a harness before, but honestly, I don't like heights very much, so the whole thing was really wild, and it took like, half a day to film the scene. By the time it was over, I was really glad. "

Emily was busy working and having the time of her life — she loved acting and had discovered that it was something at which she could really excel.

Then, a few years later, Emily got word of a new show that was looking for an actress to play Lily Truscott, the best friend of the main character. The role called for someone who was energetic, a little hyper, and full of fun and enthusiasm. Emily couldn't wait to get to the audition, where she learned the series would be called *Hannah Montana*. During the Disney Channel press conference, she told reporters about her "wild ride" of an audition. "I must have auditioned three or four times," she explained. "I kept getting called back, and I would read lines, then they'd say, 'We'll call you.' The last time I went, Miley was already cast, and they wanted me to read with her, to see how we looked together and to hear how we sounded together. Then they said, 'We'll call you!' and I thought for sure I didn't get it. But I did, and when I heard I got it, I screamed for like ten minutes, I was so excited."

Once the role was hers, Emily turned to her brother to get some acting tips, something her older sibling was always eager to share with her. He would offer her little words of advice and encouragement: don't daydream during the filming; always stay focused; look people in the eye; always be prepared and ready for anything. His advice helped her, and she was happy and proud to have a brother who was so supportive.

As soon as she stepped on the set of *Hannah Montana*, Emily knew she'd made the right decision in taking the role. The role of Lily, fun-loving, tomboyish, sporty, full of life and energy, was so much like Emily herself, that she barely had to act. And then there were the fast, tight friendships she made with the members of the cast. "I'd known Miley before, we'd been friends even before we started the show because we lived close to one another," Emily explained to *Tiger Beat* magazine. "When I first met her, I thought she was really out there, always laughing and making jokes, having a great time in her life. Then when we started working together, it was like magic, because since we already had a friendship between us, there was already a bond. It would have been terrible if we were playing best friends and in reality didn't like each other, wouldn't it? And then there was Mitchel and Jason — what great guys! They are so much fun! Mitchel and I tell each other every-thing, and Jason is like the protective big brother, always there to help out." In fact, Emily and Mitchel became so close, rumors began popping up about the two of them dating. Emily remains mum on the subject, although she has told *J-14* magazine that "Boys just complicate things. Boys are a big issue for me right now."

It's hard to say whether Emily will ever have an Oscar nomination to match her brother's, and she is definitely heading for a long career as an actress, but the talented teen has other ambitions as well. She has said she would like to be an illustrator and author one day — books have long been a passion for Emily, who loves to read and can be seen con-stantly with a book under her arm — and she has even said she might want to pursue a career in soccer, another passion. But whatever she chooses, she knows her family, and her *Hannah Montana* friends, will always be there to support her.

DID YOU KNOW . . . ?
Emily often gets insane cravings for In-N-Out burgers.

Big Brother Jason Earles

He's may be wild and goofy on *Hannah*, but in real life this talented actor is one serious guy!

Head-To-Toe Fax

Full Name:	Jason Earles
Birthday:	April 26, 1977
Birthplace:	San Diego, California
Pets:	Two cats, Timmy and Presley
Height:	5' 6"
Eyes:	Blue
FYI:	Jason is very open about having struggled with Attention Deficit Disorder when he was in middle school

Jason's Fabulous Faves

Color:	Blue
Food:	Chocolate Lucky Charms, chocolate chip cookies, and anything barbecued
TV Show:	He watches ESPN shows whenever he's at home
Sports:	Snowboarding and baseball
Actors:	Michael J. Fox and Angelina Jolie
School Subjects:	Science and math

On *Hannah Montana*, Jason Earles plays one of the goofiest roles, that of Miley's big brother Jackson, a girl-crazy, fun-loving teenager who is always getting into crazy situations and is always there to provide a joke or a laugh. So it might surprise you to know that Jason, the eldest of the four young *Hannah* cast members, is actually the most classically trained actor in the bunch, and that when it comes to performing, he is all serious, all the time.

Jason was born in San Diego, California, and he started acting in plays at a young age, winning roles in class plays. In third grade, he starred in a presentation of *Hansel & Gretel*, then began appearing in community theater productions near his hometown. Acting was a source of pride and achievement for Jason, who at a young age was diagnosed with Attention Deficit Disorder. He found that acting was a place where his energy and creativity could shine. "Having Attention Deficit Hyperactivity Disorder was something that was difficult to get a handle on, but that creative outlet, something where I could go and rehearse every afternoon for a couple of hours, gave me something to focus on and to put my energy into. I think it's so important to have something in your life — whether it's sports or music or theater — something to be really involved in, especially during middle school, which can be a hard time for many teens," Jason told PBSKids.org. "I was smaller growing up, and I wanted something that I could do and be good at." He says that he believes all kids with Attention Deficit Hyperactivity Disorder should find that special something they are good at. "It's really important for kids to get involved with something they love, because that makes it more likely that they will concentrate on it and be active in it. And it's important, too, to work with your teachers and get to know them, so they can help and support you. I had great teachers who weren't interested in sending me to the principal's office when I acted up — they wanted to find ways to help me."

Thanks to his family, his teachers, and his own hard work and determination, Jason was accepted to and attended University of Redlands in California, then moved around the country, from Montana to Oregon, working with theater groups and acting coaches. He performed in classical plays by Shakespeare, and won roles in serious plays such as *The Crucible* and *Equus*. Eventually, he moved to Los Angeles, began auditioning for roles in films and TV, and found success in TV shows like *Phil of the Future*, and movies like 2004's *National Treasure*. He was already a seasoned performer when he auditioned for the role in *Hannah Montana*.

At first Jason was nervous about accepting the role, especially when he heard that Billy Ray Cyrus would be playing Miley's dad on the show. "It was weird, but I thought, they already have this great connection and chemistry, and I wondered if I would be, like, the odd man out," he told reporters at the Disney Channel press conference. "But by the third day, Billy Ray and I were joking and we got really comfortable with each other. And Miley and I have grown to love each other — I look out for her like a big brother, and we even pick on each other like real family. So now I really do feel like an honorary Cyrus. And I'm fiercely protective of all the cast — even Billy Ray, because he was a bit new to the whole comedy thing, and sometimes he doesn't think he's funny and needs encouragement."

In order to really fit in with the family, Jason — as Jackson — had to adopt a Tennessee accent, like Miley and Billy Ray have. Luckily, Jason learned about a dozen accents while training in theater, and not only can he do a spot-on Southern accent, but he's great at doing British and Russian accents as well.

He was also called upon to be a total comedian, something that he looked forward to from the beginning. "Jackson is really fun," Jason told *USA Today*. "If something outrageous or funny is going to happen on the show, it usually happens to Jackson. He gets himself into a lot of trouble over things like girls and cars, but it's never anything really serious, it's always light and playful. But I do get the chance to do some really fun things, like falls and slapstick, which is great."

Jason loves being a member of the *Hannah Montana* crew, but like the serious young man he is, he often thinks of the future and wonders what's in store for him. He looks forward to traveling (he has always wanted to visit Ireland and other countries in Europe) and continuing to work on his acting skills. But right now, he believes he is in a great place, and he's enjoying being the big ol' goofy brother. "We knew the show was going to be good, but we didn't know it was going to be so popular," he said at the Disney press conference. "Now I find myself getting recognized more and more, and I know I'm a part of something really exciting. I'm so happy I had a chance to be a part of it, because something this special doesn't come along every day."

DID YOU KNOW . . . ?

Jason would be lost without his iPod and PlayStation.

Billy Ray Cyrus:

Superstar Dad

Miley Cyrus comes by her talent naturally. In fact, some might say, her talent is in her genes. Miley's dad, Billy Ray Cyrus, is just about one of the biggest stars country music has ever seen.

William Ray Cyrus was born in Flatlands, Kentucky. His grandfather was a Pentecostal preacher, and his father sang in a gospel quarter. But Billy's early dreams had nothing to do with music and everything to do with baseball. He attended Georgetown College on a baseball scholarship and intended to make the game his lifelong career. But fate intervened when Billy Ray, on a whim, purchased a guitar from a local store. After that, it was all about the music. Once he held the guitar in his hands, Billy Ray knew that it would be music that opened the door to his future, just as it had for his own father. He found he loved music more than anything in the world, and he became determined to succeed.

But it took many years and plenty of disappointments before Billy Ray's dream came true. On several occasions, he returned to his Kentucky home in despair, thinking he'd made the wrong choice. But he never quit, and his determination eventually paid off when he received a record deal from Mercury Records. "I was so happy I would have the chance to make a record, and I hoped people would like it," he mused to *Country Music Magazine* back in 1992.

They did.

That year, Billy's first album, *Some Gave All*, was released, and on it, there was a catchy little country dance tune called "Achy Breaky Heart." The song became a huge hit, reaching No. 1 on the country charts and making it to No. 4 on the pop music charts — not a small feat back then, when country music was a more marginalized type of music that didn't often cross over. Fans copied the Billy Ray look of torn jeans and T-shirts, men across the USA copied his signature haircut, and female fans swooned over his good looks.

The song inspired a dance craze called "line dancing," something new in country music; when dancers didn't need partners and danced instead with a long line of fellow fans. Billy Ray was awestruck. He told *Country Music Magazine*, "One day I was living out of my car, the next day I was nominated for five Grammy Awards. It happened so fast, it was spiraling out of control. Suddenly people were dressing like me, the song was everywhere. I couldn't believe it."

The album had more than one hit — "Some Gave All," "Where'm I Gonna Live," and "It Could've Been Me" all flew up the charts. But wherever Billy Ray went, fans were sure to scream for "Achy Breaky Heart" — it's still his most popular song.

Billy Ray released several more albums, including *It Won't Be the Last*, *Storm in the Heartland*, and the critical hit *Trail of Tears*, but while he retained legions of fans, these albums didn't do as well as his first. Billy Ray retreated to the safe haven provided by his family, including baby Destiny Hope, born in 1992 when "Achy Breaky Heart" was making him a star. "When the famous life began to fade away, I reconnected with my real life, and with my family," he explained to *Country Music Magazine*. "I had always been a family man, but sometimes when you're experiencing fame, you forget about what's important in your life. I was always able to stay true to myself because I had my family to support and love me."

But while Billy Ray may have made a quick stage exit from music superstardom, he never stopped working. He continued to record albums, and he began to explore a career in acting. In 2001, he auditioned for a role for the PAX series *Doc*, and amazed the producers with his sincerity and true acting talent. He also made guest appearances on *The Nanny* and eventually appeared in the musical *Annie Get Your Gun* in Canada. And when Disney announced they were seeking actors for roles in a show called *Hannah Montana*, Billy Ray was the first in line — the network loved the idea of pairing Miley and her real life dad in the sitcom. Now he's won a new generation of fans. "Every now and then, I get young fans shouting, 'There's Hannah's dad'," he exclaimed to *USA Today*. "I couldn't be prouder of Miley, and I'm proud of myself, too, because I know I do the best job I can on the show."

For Miley, working with her father has been a wonderful experience, and even though he once discouraged her from seeking a show-business career, he is now her number one advisor. "It's cool to learn from him and to have him guide me along," she told *USA Today*. "He always gives me the courage to face whatever comes. He always tells me, 'You can do anything you want, just keep going. You're going to make it.'"

Today, the Cyrus pair not only works together on *Hannah Montana*, they also share the stage musically. Miley backed up her dad vocally on a song called "Stand" from his latest album, *Wanna Be Your Joe*, and the two harmonized on "I Learned From You," which you can hear on the *Hannah Montana* soundtrack. Billy Ray could not be happier of how his own life turned out, or prouder of his very special daughter. "For an ol' boy from Flatlands, life is pretty good," he said, smiling at reporters at the Disney Channel press conference. "I hope life will always be as good for Miley."

Crushable Cody Linley!

Miley has a crush on Cody, and so do his many fans. Here's what you need to know about the guy who stole Hannah's heart!

Head-To-Toe Fax

Full Name: Cody Martin Linley
Birthday: November 20, 1989
Birthplace: Denton, Texas
Family: Cody's mom, Catherine, and his dad, Lou, have been separated since Cody was 12. He has four siblings: three step-brothers named Ben, Scotty, and Jason, and a brother named Jimmy
Eyes: Green
Height: 5' 8"

Cody's Fabulous Faves

Color: Green
Sports: Basketball
Actors: Kevin Bacon and Leonardo DiCaprio
Music: Country and rock
Food: Steaks and Hawaiian-style pizza
Drinks: Orange juice
Gum: Orbit

This past year on *Hannah Montana*, Miley Stewart developed a head-over-heels crush on Jake Ryan, an actor and teen idol who just happens to attend school with Miley, Oliver, and Lily. Although she'd had crushes on other guys, this one was different — she'd been thinking about nothing but Jake since he first appeared on the scene. And they shared a rather up-and-down relationship, since there were plenty of other girls with their eyes on Jake, too.

In real life, Miley Cyrus couldn't have been happier when she read the script, which had her receiving her first kiss from Jake (played by the talented Cody Linley), the gorgeous heartthrob who'd made several guest appearances on *Hannah Montana* before the big smooching scene. In fact, Miley told *Teen* magazine that she had a real-life crush on Cody. "Yes, I have to admit it," she said. "I have a total crush on him. He doesn't like me, but I don't really care, because he's so fun to look at. I love being on the set with him, he's fun, down-to-earth, and he's hot!"

The actor she was talking about, 18-year-old Cody, is a lot more than just a handsome face and a smooth talker, (his signature line on *Hannah* is, "Dude, I slayed you once, I can slay you again"). He also hap-

pens to be a terrific young actor who's been performing since he was a young tyke in Texas. Cody's energy and sweet face got him noticed by casting directors. Directors of commercials and TV shows were impressed with his ability to work hard, even at a young age, and with his knack for working well with other actors. But while he was a working actor, he and his parents made the decision to keep him in public school, where his teachers and friends were completely supportive. His teachers at Huffness Middle School remember that when he was in the fifth grade, Cody tried out for a part in *Harry Potter*, and was totally devastated when he didn't win the role. But they praised him for the fact that he never once thought of giving up.

In 1998, Cody made his movie debut in the film *Still Holding On: The Legend of Cadillac Jack*. He was eight when he made his big-screen movie debut, playing Spit in *My Dog Skip*, and he soon began acting constantly, taking small roles in *Miss Congeniality* and *Cheaper by the Dozen*. By this time, his parents gave in and moved with him and the family to California, so he could pursue his acting career with full force.

In 2006, Cody won legions of fans when he appeared in the film *Hoot*. He played Mullet Fingers, a wild boy with a good heart — a rebel whose cause is saving the environment and protecting the owls that live near his home. Cody was excited to be a part of a film that carried such an important message, one that has become very important to him in real life as well.

Cody has had some experience working with the Disney Channel, guest-starring on shows like *That's So Raven* and *The Cheetah Girls 2*. But it has been *Hannah Montana* that has made him a household name, and that smooching scene that's brought him the most attention, especially from his costar, Miley. "I was really looking forward to doing the kissing scene, even though honestly, when you're filming a kiss on TV, it's not even a little romantic with all those people watching," Miley told *Teen* magazine. "I still knew it was going to be my favorite scene of the season, and it was. And he was the perfect kisser. His lips are like velvet and he's totally cute. He's like an angel. At one point, they weren't filming anymore, but I made Cody think they were so I could kiss him one more time."

Cody definitely enjoys the attention from fans, and from Miley, but he hasn't let his fame go to his head, and deep-down, he's remained a true Texas gentleman. "I constantly go back and forth from Texas to California," he told *Tiger Beat* magazine. "I feel fortunate, because I get to live in the same town as my grandparents and my parents. My family is very important to me, and I like to have that connection to family that comes from living at home in Texas. I work in Los Angeles, and I love it there, but home is really where my heart is, in Texas."

FUN CODY FACT!

Cody is completely obsessed with his guitar, and whenever he gets a free moment, he can be found practicing. All his friends and family know that if they can't reach him on his cell phone, it's because he's got it stashed away so he can practice in total silence and concentration.

DID YOU KNOW . . . ?

Miley has had crushes on Chad Michael Murray, Ryan Cabrera, and Jesse McCartney.

Hannah Music

Take 1 The Soundtrack Hits The Roof

On October 24, 2006, Miley Cyrus and Hannah Montana broke a musical record when "their" CD, *Hannah Montana* soundtrack, flew to the number one spot on the music charts and sold over 281,000 copies in one week. Why was that record breaking? Because until that week, there had never been a TV soundtrack album that had sold so many CDs in such a short amount of time. In addition, the CD earned top spots on *Billboard*'s Children's Chart and Soundtrack Chart. An article in *Billboard* magazine about the soundtrack said, "Hannah Montana isn't the first fictional character to appear on a *Billboard* chart, but the teenage singer, portrayed by Miley Cyrus is the first act to have six songs debut on the *Billboard* Top 100 in the same week."

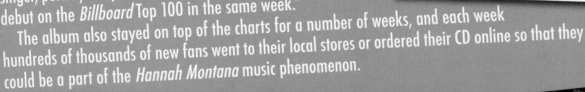

The album also stayed on top of the charts for a number of weeks, and each week hundreds of thousands of new fans went to their local stores or ordered their CD online so that they could be a part of the *Hannah Montana* music phenomenon.

Take 2 Hannah Hits The Road!

With the success of the soundtrack album, it wasn't long before Miley found herself in talks discussing a concert tour, but with her performing as Hannah Montana, not as Miley. The dates were set, and Miley learned she would be the opening act for the Cheetah Girls, another one of Disney's hotter-than-hot groups. "It was for 23 shows," Miley told *J-14* magazine. "It was so great. I would perform a few songs early on, then I would come back and do a song called 'Girls Just Wanna Have Fun' with the Cheetah Girls." After a few weeks, Miley went back to begin filming another season of *Hannah Montana*, and *High School Musical*'s

Vanessa Anne Hudgens stepped in for the Cheetah Girls' tour.

Although Miley had a blast on the tour, and enjoyed meeting fans across the country, she was also keeping a secret — she longed for the day when she, Miley, would step out onto the stage on her own. "I love Hannah, but I can't wait to be known as Miley, the singer," she told *USA Today*. "My music is a little different than Hannah's. It's more personal, telling people who I am and speaking to fans through my songs. My music is a mixture that reflects me, a little country and a little rock."

Take 3 Hannah And Miley Hit The Big Time!

Fans could hardly wait for a new album from Hannah, and they got it on June 26, 2007 — only this time, Hannah wasn't alone.

True to her dream, Miley and Hannah both got a chance to sing their songs on *Hannah Montana 2 — Best of Both Worlds*. A two-CD set, the first CD features ten songs from the TV series, and the second is a solo Miley CD with songs written by Miley herself. "I am so stoked, I'm so excited," she said in her press release from Hollywood Records. "It's introducing fans to me, to Miley, which is so cool, and still giving them the chance to hear Hannah, who definitely rocks."

No one was surprised when Miley began writing her own songs — dad Billy Ray said the two had always written songs together, ever since Miley was young. But fans were amazed at how strong the songs were, how personal, and most importantly, how good they were. The album, just like its predecessor, flew up the charts, and fans began to wait patiently for the day that Miley and Hannah would perform their new songs, together.

Take 4 The Tour Hits New Heights!

In the warm, waning summer days of August 2007, word began to leak that Miley was going to have her dream come true. A new tour was planned, this time starring Hannah Montana and Miley Cyrus, each one performing for half of one enormous concert that was sure to be the hit of the year.

Tickets went on sale, and if you blinked, you missed 'em — they sold out in seconds! No one was prepared for the number of fans who wanted to see their idol in person. In some cities, second and third shows were added. "We couldn't believe it!" Miley told newspapers in St. Louis, Missouri, the city that would sponsor the opening night of Miley's concert. "We just couldn't believe the way the tickets sold out. I hope everyone who wants to see me was able to get a ticket, because I can't wait to see everyone out there!"

Miley & Hannah LIVE!

On a warm evening in October, 2007, in St. Louis, Missouri, there was only one place to be — at the Scottsdale Center for the opening night of the Miley Cyrus/Hannah Montana tour called, most appropriately, Best of Both Worlds.

And it truly was the best of both because the audience would get the chance to see Miley performing as Hannah Montana, and as Miley herself. It was the chance for fans to see "both" sides of the superstar. In interviews before opening night, Miley told reporters, "Of course I'm Miley, but Hannah is such an important part of me and my life. It made sense to give audiences the chance to see us both perform."

And the night would be extra special for fans, who would also get to see the popular Jonas Brothers performing as the concert's opening act. The brothers, who had recently appeared on a special episode of *Hannah Montana*, were excited to have the chance to perform their song, "We Got the Party," (the song they performed on the show) live, with Hannah.

DID YOU KNOW . . . ?

The first song Miley ever sang was "L-O-V-E" from *The Parent Trap*.

Opening Night

As the lights fell and the audience chanted "We love you, Miley," there was a charge of electricity in the air. Fans knew they were about the see an awesome performance, and they were ready to sing along and cheer for their favorite singer.

As Hannah, Miley didn't just step onto the stage; she was lowered from the ceiling in an illuminated cube. She was welcomed by thousands of screaming fans — and the screaming didn't stop for one second during the 75-minute show. A blond-wigged Miley, as Hannah, began her performance with her hit, "Rock Star," then happily greeted her fans, shouting, "Hey everybody! I hope you're ready to have a great time!"

Hannah was all about the music, but she was also all about the clothes. After finishing a song, she would bound offstage to change costumes, calling out, "I'll be back as soon as I change my dress!" The audience was entertained by her back-up dancers, a group choreographed by Kenny Ortega, the guy behind the dance moves on *High School Musical*. Each time she reappeared, the audience roared its approval of her new outfit, and she burst into giggles before belting out another tune.

When Hannah's portion of the concert was done, the stage lit up with fireworks that brightened the arena and sizzled across the stage. The Jonas Brothers returned to sing their biggest hits, "Kids of the Future" and "Year 3000," then stood back and smiled as an elevator lifted Miley up through the floor and back to her fans. Miley enchanted her fans with her hit, "Start All Over," then gushed, "I could not dream of a better way to start the 'Best of Both Worlds' tour. Thank you so much for being here tonight with me. I love you!"

The crowd went crazy over Miley, and when she finished her part of the concert, there was another blaze of fireworks, and pink and lavender streamers filled the arena. But the audience wouldn't let her leave just yet —they demanded another song, and Miley happily returned to the stage with a smile on her face. "This one is for my grandpa," she told the audience, as she picked up her guitar and performed "I Miss You," a quiet, thoughtful song she had written for her late grandfather.

When the night was over, Miley waved good-bye to her fans, but she couldn't help but take one last look at the audience, smiling a mile wide and jumping up and down a bit before heading back-stage. "I love being able to sing and dance and write songs," she said after the show had ended. "It's the fans who give me a chance to do that. I will always love the fans, because without them, I wouldn't be here. This is all for them."

Adventures With Miley!

Miley has already been a huge success on TV and in music — can movies be far behind?

Disney Studios are currently working to bring Miley to the big screen, with none other than Raven Symone of *That's So Raven* as her costar, in a remake of the 1987 classic comedy hit, *Adventures in Babysitting*.

The original movie starred Elisabeth Shue as a high school senior who is bored silly by her job as a baby-sitter to a group of bratty kids. But one night, while watching the bunch, she gets a call from a friend who needs her help, and she has no choice but to bring all the kids with her. Together they face a slew of crazy situations and, eventually, save the day and the friend.

The new film, which is tentatively titled *Further Adventures in Babysitting*, might star Miley as the babysitter, and Raven as the friend in need. The two have worked together before, most notably in Disney's awesome combination show *That's So Suite Life of Hannah Montana*. But both are looking forward to working together again, and this time in a comedy movie that fans are bound to absolutely love.

DID YOU KNOW . . . ?

If Miley could costar with anyone in the world, it would be Orlando Bloom — although she admits she might swoon first; he's one of her celebrity crushes!